Bears Don't Read!

Emma Chichester Clark

HarperCollins *Children's Books*

First published in hardback in Great Britain by
HarperCollins Children's Books in 2014

1 3 5 7 9 10 8 6 4 2

ISBN: 978-0-00-742518-1

HarperCollins Children's Books is a division of
HarperCollins Publishers Ltd.

Visit our website at: www.harpercollins.co.uk

Printed in China

Mayfield School
This book belongs
to
George

Most days, George sat on a bench at the edge of the woods and stared out at the distant hills. He wondered about Life.

Oh, life is lovely, he thought. Tra-la-la and all that! But is this it? he wondered. Is this all there is?

His brothers and sisters never wondered about anything. They were perfectly happy chatting, fishing – doing the usual bear things – and telling the same old stories over and over again.

But George was bored. He didn't want to do the usual bear things anymore. He wanted other things. But *what?* he wondered.

Then, one day, as George was strolling through the forest, he found a book lying beneath a tree.

Somebody must have lost it, he thought. How interesting! Inside it were pictures of a bear – just like him.

On the other pages there were lots and lots of words.

Each one, even the tiny ones, is saying *something*, he thought. If only I knew what it was... and this bear is having an exciting life, not like mine! George sighed.

But then, he had a brilliant idea!

He rushed home to tell the others.

"I'm going to town to find the owner of this book and ask them to teach me to read!" he said.

"You don't want to go there!" said his brother. "They don't like bears in town."

"But I want to learn to *read!*" said George.

"That's just silly!" said his sister. "Bears don't read! Why can't you be happy doing normal bear things?"

But George
would not be
put off. He
waved goodbye
and headed
towards the long
road into town
with the book
under his arm.

George walked for a whole day and a whole night, stopping to rest on a grassy hill under the sparkling sky.

Before he slept he opened the book again and gazed at the words. Already he felt that the world was a more interesting place.

The next morning, George rose with the sun and by midday he could see the town in the distance. He smiled. It looked lovely.

There must be so many people who know how to read there, he thought, and lots of new stories they can tell me.

But when he arrived everyone was running! Some were even screaming! "WAIT!" cried George.

He showed the book to a woman rushing by. "Do you know whose this is?" he asked. "It's from the schooool!" she shrieked and pointed to the red building.

"BEAR!" somebody shouted. "Call the police!"
How peculiar! thought George as he walked
towards the school.

Inside the school, there was complete silence. Where was everybody?

George peered over the desk.

"Hello!" he said, but there
was nobody there.

Suddenly, there was a shout.
"Freeze! Hands above your head!"
George was surrounded by policemen!
"What's the matter?" he asked nervously.

"You're a gigantic, great grizzly bear!" shouted the Chief of Police. "That's the matter!" They moved towards him, holding up their shields.

"I don't want any trouble!"
said the Chief.

George didn't want any trouble either.

It wasn't his fault he was a
gigantic, great grizzly bear!

He held the book tightly in his paw.

Just then, the doors burst open and in walked a little girl called Clementine with her mother.

"Hey!" cried Clementine. "That's *my* book... *and that's the bear in my book!*"

"This is a dangerous animal!" roared the Chief.

"STAND BACK!"

"He doesn't look
dangerous to me!"
said Clementine.

"NO!" said George "I'm not
that sort of bear at all! I was
just hoping someone could
teach me to read!"

"SILENCE!"
roared the Chief.

But Clementine wasn't listening.

"I'm learning to read," she said.
"We could learn together, couldn't we, Mum?"

Clementine's mother looked at George.
She could see he was a perfectly nice
sort of bear.

"I don't see why not!" she said.

"So you'll take responsibility for this bear, will you, madam?" asked the Chief.

"Certainly!" said Clementine's mother. "And there's no need to shout!"

She held out her hand to George.

"Very pleased to meet you," she said.
"Delighted to meet you too!" said George.

George moved into the summerhouse at the end of Clementine's garden and each day, after school, Clementine showed him everything she'd learned.

It wasn't long before George knew all the letters of the alphabet.

D d
B b
A a
C c
H h
F f
T t

George didn't find reading easy at first. Even though he tried hard he often made mistakes but, luckily, Clementine was a kind and patient teacher.

Sometimes the Chief came to see how they were getting on. He brought a book of his favourite poetry to read aloud to George.

Then one day, Clementine said,
"I bet you can read this whole book now,
all by yourself!"

George opened it and began,

"Once upon a time,
there was a large
brown bear who
found a book lying
under a tree..."

He read the whole book, all the way to the end.
"Bravo!" said Clementine. "We knew you could do it!"

And for George – that was just the beginning.